For Jon-Jo with love
M.I.

First published 1989 by
Walker Books Ltd, 87 Vauxhall Walk
London SE11 5HJ

This edition published 2002

4 6 8 10 9 7 5 3

© 1989 Mick Inkpen

Printed in Hong Kong

British Library Cataloguing in Publication Data:
a catalogue record for this book is
available from the British Library

ISBN 0-7445-8287-3

Jojo's Revenge!

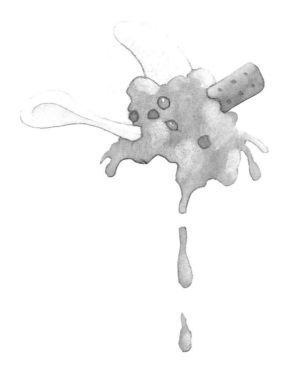

Written and illustrated by
MICK INKPEN

WALKER BOOKS
AND SUBSIDIARIES
LONDON • BOSTON • SYDNEY

Like all babies Jojo
was squeezed and
squashed and passed
around a lot.
Like pass the parcel.

Everyone wanted to
prod him to make
him smile.
Or poke their fingers
into his mouth to
see if he had grown
any teeth.

People would knit him cardigans that were too big.
Or too small.
The silliest one had a matching pom-pom hat with ear flaps.

And though his cot was full of furry animals, the things he really wanted were always out of reach.

At night, just as Jojo was beginning to enjoy a good yell, someone would always find a way to stop him.

And once, even
his mum got cross
with him for filling
his nappy.
"Oh Jojo," she said,
"not now!"

So one day, to get his own back, Jojo decided that instead of eating his dinner, he would wear it!

After this there was
no stopping him.
Every day Jojo managed
to try on his breakfast,
his dinner or his tea.
"It's because he's like
me," said Grandpa.
"He's artistic!"

Jojo's mum bought
him some face
paints to play with.
But Jojo ignored them.
He preferred to paint
with porridge.

Then one day Jojo's
mum went out,
leaving his grandpa
to look after him.
"Try not to let him
make too much mess
with his dinner,"
she said.

When she got back
she was amazed.
Jojo's plate was empty
and there was not a
single scrap of food
on him.
"Grandpa! How did
you do it?" she said.

"Like this!"
said Jojo's grandpa.

MICK INKPEN says of the story of *Jojo's Revenge* that
"It is the lot of all babies to be squidged, and the solemn
duty of all friends and relations to be the squidgers!"

Mick Inkpen is the author and illustrator of many books
for children, including the popular titles about Kipper the dog,
which have been adapted for a long-running and successful
television series; *Threadbear*, which won the Children's Book
Award; and *Penguin Small,* which won the Illustrated Children's
Book of the Year. He says that the inspiration for *JoJo's Revenge*
came from a combination of his youngest nephew, Jon-Jo,
and "a dinner-wearing incident from my own dim past".
Mick has two grown-up children and lives in Suffolk
with his wife, Debbie.